The Girl in the Cave

~*A Short Thriller*~

by Tomika Reid

The Girl in the Cave

Copyright © 2021 by Tomika Y. Reid

ISBN-13
Paperback- 978-0-9975290-6-7

Library of Congress Control Number
2024916305

Published by Tomika Reid

Cover Design by Tomika Reid and Ronald Comeau

Illustrations by Ronald Comeau

This book was printed in the United States of America.

To My Readers,

Your unwavering support means everything.

Thank you for having faith in me and taking the

time to support my work continually.

Life is a journey, and yet, it's a journey well

worth it.

It's supporters like you who help dreams come

true.

You are amazing!

Always follow your dream, and no matter what,

don't give up on yourself.

Love & Light,
Tomika Y. Reid

for the young female driver

Alone on the road can be dark and scary,

drifty and dreary.

You are hoping for the best,

unknowingly

for what might happen next.

Imagine being put to the test in the darkness.

~ Tomika Y. Reid

THE GIRL IN THE CAVE

After the bell rang. Lisa could not wait to meet up with her girls, Sasha and Kim. Lisa was too excited; she missed her girls. Lisa, Sasha, and Kim were all best friends. They grew up together. Lisa could not wait to see them. They were only away from each other for three periods, and it was now lunchtime—a time for them to catch up on some girl talk and to talk about this Friday night's party.

Lisa does not usually party, she's the one who would rather stay home and watch movies. Sasha and Kim enjoyed partying—they enjoyed having all types of fun, and when it came down to her girls, Lisa was ride or die.

When Lisa saw Kim, they greeted each other with a hug.

"Girl, are we partying Friday night, or what?" asked Kim.

Sasha overheard walking down the hall.

"Hell yeah!" she shouted filled with excitement, as she embraced her girls with a hug.

Lisa, Sasha, and Kim talked about any and everything. The girls have been this way since public school. Lisa expressed how happy she was seeing Sasha and Kim during their lunch break but was not too excited about partying Friday night.

"Lisa, why do you look unbothered?" asked Sasha.

The girls laughed as they walked from their lockers to sit down in the lunchroom.

"I don't know you guys. I really don't feel up to partying on Friday," said Lisa.

"It's only Monday, Lisa. You'll change your mind by then," said Sasha.

Whose party is it...? What time are we talking...? What are we wearing...? I mean, who's going to be there?" asked Lisa.

First of all, the party starts 11:00 p.m. Troy from the senior's basketball team is giving the party. Josh, Levi, and Tony will be there, and you know who I can't wait to see, my fine-ass ex James. He's going to be there, and plenty of others.

Oh, and we can get there by midnight—
everybody should be there by then," said Sasha.

"Well, you know who I can't wait to see,
Trooooy!" said Kim.

"Girl, why you say it like that...? Trooooy,
with the extra o's," said Sasha, as she laughed
along with Lisa and Kim.

"I don't like him, I mean, I do, then I don't,"
said Kim.

"Which one is it...you do, or you don't?"
asked Sasha while laughing.

"He's cute and all, but there will be plenty of
other girls there he'll be looking at...he won't
pay me no mind...at least I get to see him at his
party, though," said Kim.

"Girl, you are cute, beautiful, and got it going on, not to mention a smart, intelligent young lady, my best friend. Besides, he cordially invited all three of us. So, he might be looking at you," said Lisa. Kim started to blush.

"Well, I'll meet y'all there since I'm closer," said Sasha.

"I guess I'll be picking you up then, Kim," said Lisa nonchalantly.

"All right then, we are in there!" Sasha rejoiced.

"See how fast you changed your mind?" Sasha asked sarcastically.

"Girl, I'm only going because my girls are going, and I don't want y'all in there by y'all-selves," Lisa said as she chuckled.

"Girl, you know you will miss us calling every second, making sure we're all right," said Kim.

"Right, talking about what y'all doing…y'all okay?" said Sasha.

"But wait, what are we wearing?" asked Lisa.

"Whatever's cute in my closet, that's what I'm wearing," said Kim. "Well, I don't know yet, I have to see," responded Lisa.

"Well, I'm putting on whatever's sexy in my closet, maybe my black bodycam dress with the sides out, my black stilettos, and my hair in a bun because you know I must look extra cute for James," said Sasha.

"Girl, isn't that your ex?" Lisa said sarcastically. "Yes, but you know he still wants me," said Sasha. "And you know you still want him," added Kim.

The girls laughed. One thing about Sasha, Lisa, and Kim is that they all had a sense of humor. They laughed with each other about almost everything. Lunch break was over by the time they finished laughing and talking.

"I'll see you girls later," Lisa said as she uprose from the table to go to her next class. They hugged each other and departed.

"Hi Kim, you still coming to my party Friday night?" asked Troy while he and Kim passed each other in the hallway.

"I wouldn't miss it even if I wanted to," says Kim, with tantalizing eyes and a smile.

Kim knew she liked Troy, and Troy seemed to like her. When school was over, the girls met up to go home. Sasha went her way. Lisa and Kim rode together.

"Girl, guess who I saw in the hallway?" asked Kim in a surprised tone.

"Who?" Lisa replied.

"Troy, we saw each other passing through…he inclined if I was still coming to his party."

"And what did you say?" asked Lisa.

"I told him I wouldn't miss it even if I wanted to," said Kim as she chuckled.

"Girl, stop… He likes you, and you like him. I told you he might be looking at you, too," the girls chuckled.

"I just cannot wait until Friday night to see how he acts," said Kim.

"Well, we shall see," responded Lisa.

"Yes, we shall see," said Kim with a smile. She could not wait.

Suddenly, Lisa slammed on the brakes abruptly to avoid hitting the black car coming out of the gas station. The driver looked at Lisa.

Lisa looked back at the driver with an angry stare. The driver drove off like nothing happened.

"Did you see that...? He didn't even stop coming out of the gas station—he could've caused an accident, then he looked at me as if I was in the wrong," Lisa said, with a sign of irritation.

"Girl, it's some crazy people in the world today. They don't care about nobody but themselves," said Kim while shaking her head.

After a few days had gone by, it was finally Friday.

"Today came quick, y'all know we should get off this phone and start getting ready," said Lisa while on the three-way call with Sasha and Kim.

"Girl, we got until tonight," Sasha responded.

"Sasha, you are the main one who takes forever to get ready; you should already be ready!" Lisa exclaimed.

"No, not me, darling, that's Kim, watch and see, she's gonna have you waiting on her tonight," said Sasha laughingly.

"Don't turn the tables on me, Sasha," said Kim.

"Kim, you better be ready when I call you to say I'm on my way. That's all I'm saying, now goodbye ladies, see y'all in a few," said Lisa. The girls laughed at each other and hung up.

They spent the rest of the day preparing for the party tonight, trying on every sexy outfit they could find in their closet.

They did their makeup and their hair and were ready to go.

Lisa looked over at her dresser and picked up a picture of her parents; "Mom and Dad, I wish you were here," Lisa said as she kissed the picture frame of her mom and dad.

Lisa self-observed herself in the mirror, trying to figure out what she had on was good enough. She knew how her friends would dress, but she did not want to wear anything that would make her feel and look uncomfortable.

"Hmm, I guess I look good," Lisa said while dialing Sasha's number.

"Are you ready…? It's 12:05 a.m.," Lisa asked.

"Girl, I'm still trying to find something to wear; you know I have to look good," said Sasha.

"Girl, bye, I'm calling Kim to let her know I'm on my way," said Lisa.

"Okay, bye, see you in a few," Sasha replied. The girls hung up.

"I'm on my way. I hope you're ready," Lisa said to Kim when she answered the phone.

"Yeah, I'm ready," Kim responded, sounding iffy.

"All right, I'm on my way now," Lisa said knowingly; Kim was lying about being ready.

When Lisa got to Kim's house, she was half dressed, and makeup was half done.

"Girl, I thought you were ready…? I knew you were lying." Lisa chuckled.

"I know Lisa. I know. The only thing left for me to do is comb my hair down and put on some eyeliner and lipstick. Oh, and throw this outfit on. We will be out of here in no time," said Kim.

"Girl, bye," Lisa said as they both chuckled.

Lisa waited for Kim. Then her phone rang, it was Sasha.

"Where y'all at…? I'm here, and it's packed!

"Girl, I'm still at Kim's house…she's still getting ready," Lisa said nonchalantly.

"Girl, you could never be on the time," Sasha shouted through the speakerphone.

"I'm coming, I'm coming, I'm almost ready," said Kim.

"Hurry up, bye!" Sasha said as she hung up the phone.

Kim and Lisa did not get to the party 'till about 12:40 a.m. By the time they arrived, everyone was drunk and dancing everywhere.

The girls partied like they never partied before. Sasha was drunk already, and Kim was well on her way.

Lisa did not drink much; she knew she had to

drive her and Kim home.

After partying, Lisa and Kim decided to leave. Sasha wanted to stay with James. She was having too much fun. Kim was too, but Lisa was ready to go.

"Party over here," said Sasha with her hands up high.

"We are leaving!" Lisa yelled over the music.

"Party over here, bye," said Sasha, leaning over to hug her girls.

"Let's go!" shouted Lisa as she walked away.

Lisa walked, and Kim followed, but before she could walk out the door, Troy pulled her by the arm.

"Where are you going?" he asked.

"Lisa's my ride, so I have to go, and besides, she can't drive home alone," said Kim while pulling away.

Troy's face looked like a sad puppy; he did not want Kim to leave.

"I'll catch up with you tomorrow. Perhaps we can get dinner or something." Kim smiled; she could not believe what Troy just said to her.

"Kim let's go!" yelled Lisa from the car.

"Coming," Kim replied, staggering to the passengers' side.

She was too drunk, and as soon as Lisa pulled off, Kim threw up.

"Oh, hell no…! Damn Kim, you don't need to drink anymore," said Lisa.

"I need water," said Kim, as she groaned. Luckily, Lisa was driving slowly; Kim threw up almost entirely outside of the car, but it did not miss the door as she flung it open.

"Where would we stop this time of night to get a water…? You should've taken one from the party," said Lisa.

"I didn't see any, not that I was looking for one at the time anyway, Lisa," said Kim, groaning continuously.

Lisa saw a gas station, the same gas station from the other day. She was hesitating to go in, but Kim needed water badly.

"Are you okay?" Lisa asked while pulling into the gas station.

"Not really," Kim replied.

"No more drinking for you," said Lisa as she opened the car door.

While in line waiting to pay for the items, Lisa noticed the same guy who almost caused an accident the other day coming out of the bathroom. When he walked past her, she smelled pure beer, like he immersed himself in a beer bath; this guy was dirty and looked as though he was up to no good.

Lisa did not pay him any mind; she paid for the water and a pack of gum and walked out of the store, only to notice a car next to hers. As she got closer, she saw that it was Troy.

"What a surprise… Did you follow us, and how come you are not at your party?" asked Lisa while opening the car door.

Lisa gave Kim a bottle of water. She drank it like she never had anything to drink before as it spilled out the sides of her mouth. Kim was drunk and thirsty.

"Ooh, this is so embarrassing," she said as she looked at Troy.

"I'll take you home," Troy said to Kim.

"No, I got her," Lisa said as she put her seat belt on.

"I'll be okay, Lisa," Kim replied.

"Are you crazy…? I'm not letting you go with him… Why would I let you ride with him in your condition?"

"No," said Lisa, looking displeased.

"I'll be okay," said Kim.

"She'll be okay, Lisa. I won't bite her—I just figured I can save you a trip. You can go straight home. It's late. I thought about it when you both were leaving. Listen, I'm just a good brother trying to do a good deed, that's all. I won't touch her, I promise," said Troy as he clasped his hands together.

"Look he won't touch me, he said it, but if he does, I'll make sure we'll get him," said Kim, as she smiled.

"All right, Kim, are you sure?" asked Lisa while looking at Kim disapprovingly.

"Yes, I'll be fine. I'll call you soon as he drops me off, I promise—love you," said Kim.

"Okay, I'll be waiting for your call, and I love you, too," said Lisa, as she leaned in to hug Kim with a smile.

"Troy, you better get my girl home safely," said Lisa.

She did not want Kim to go with him, though she knew how much Kim liked Troy. Also, Lisa knew Troy was not a bad boy either; he meant well, when he said he just wanted to do a good deed.

Lisa did not start driving until she made sure Kim was safe and buckled in. She followed Troy's car until he made a left at the light. She continued straight ahead.

Lisa noticed a black car behind her with a broken headlight, she continually looked in the rear-view mirror to ensure the driver would not ride her tail too close.

"POP" … Lisa was scared after hearing the *pop* sound. She continued to drive slowly; the driver behind her drove past amazingly fast while she was trying to figure out where the sound was coming from.

Lisa wished it was nothing serious, but after hearing the flapping sound from the deflated tire hitting the road, she panicked.

"*NOOO!* … It's the wrong time for this. Shit!" Lisa angrily said, as she got out of the car to see which tire was busted.

She checked the front two tires. They were fine, and just as she walked to the rear left side, she noticed her tire busted.

Lisa reached into her car to get her cell phone. She did not want to call a toll truck because it was extremely late. She called Sasha—no answer. She called 911, but before she could state the emergency, she noticed a white car pulling over on the opposite side of the road, so she hung up. Lisa dropped her cell phone in the car seat when she heard a voice, "Hey there, young lady, I see you have a busted tire... I can change it for you at no cost if you have a spare," said the unknown man as he exited his vehicle, then started walking across the two-way street towards her.

Lisa was desperate and scared, yet happy to have someone to help. She accepted his offer. Unaware that her impulsive behavior could change her life in the next minute or two.

"Yes, I have a spare, thank God," said Lisa while walking to open the trunk. After moving the items around in the trunk to reach the spare tire, Lisa detected the beer smell.

She then turned around only to find that the man who offered to help her was the same man from the gas station. He changed his shirt, he wore a cap hat, and his car was different; the unknown man disguised himself, and although he did, the smell was unforgettable.

"Wait, aren't you the man I saw from the store at the gas station, the same man who almost caused me to have an accident the other day?" Lisa asked fearfully while slowly walking backward to get into her car.

"Ma'am, I don't know what you're talking about… I'm just trying to help you," he said as he followed Lisa step by step.

Lisa got into her car and closed and locked

the doors. She was panicking while trying to find her phone. She then realized she was sitting on it. Lisa grabbed her phone for face recognition, but the phone was taking too long to capture her face.

"Please don't hurt me, please don't hurt me, I just want to go home," said Lisa shakingly, awaiting the phone to capture her face.

"Open the door," said the unknown man as he banged on the car window. "I'm not going to hurt you," he said.

Finally, Lisa was recognized but before she could press the emergency button the unknown man punched his hand through the car window, knocking her unconscious.

He opened the door, picked her up to the trunk of his car, and locked her in. The unknown man drove off. He played loud music while smoking a cigarette. He left Lisa's car and belongings abandoned on the road. He took Lisa to his house, not too far from where the abduction took place.

The unknown man's house was at the end of the road in the back where there was only one house, tall trees, and two cars, a black car and the white car he was driving. Before the unknown man took Lisa inside the house, he rearranged both cars to put the one with Lisa in the back, and then he checked to see if his mother was not outside her room.

The unknown man and his elderly mother lived together. His mother didn't come out of the room unless it was to eat or use the bathroom. When he saw that the coast was clear, he went to get Lisa from the car. He picked her up and brought her into the house, tapped the wall with his shoulder, and it turned into a revolving door. Behind that door was a cave.

The unknown man walked down the cave to a door, and through that door was a dark room; he walked over to another wall, tapped his shoulder on it, and ended up in a small room. At this point, they were deep in the cave underneath the house.

Lisa woke up screaming while he was chaining her to the pole.

"*LET ME OUT PLEASE LET ME OUT! SOMEBODY HELP ME! PLEASE! I JUST WANT TO GO HOME! SOMEBODY!*" Lisa continued to scream uncontrollably.

The unknown man left Lisa's helpless body there as she squirmed on the floor with the little bit of strength she had as she cried out for help.

A few hours later, the unknown man brought Lisa food and water. Lisa started to scream again, "*LET ME LOOSE!*" she shouted.

"No one can hear you; I'm not go-o-o-o-ing to hurt you, I-I-I just think you are bea-u-ti-ful, I-I-I-I just want you here with me, he said as he stuttered and rubbed her face with his hand and forced her to drink some water.

"Please let me go," said Lisa before drinking the water. "I can't let you go," he said.

Lisa spit the water out into his face. He grew angry; he became infuriated, grabbed her, let her go, and left.

Lisa continued to cry and scream while still chained to the pole, but no one could hear her.

She didn't know she was way deep underground in a cave.

Lisa lay there chained for several hours; she began to stretch her feet to bring the food and the rest of the water toward her weak body.

She knew if she ate and drank the water, it would give her the energy she needed. Lisa did not want the food but didn't have a choice. While stretching to get the food and water, she overheard the unknown man coming, so she stopped.

"Can I use the bathroom?" asked Lisa. He gave Lisa a bucket to use. She couldn't do much with her hands chained to the pole.

Lisa shook her chained hands against the pole to get his attention.

"No, please don't touch me," Lisa said as she moved back when he tried to help her.

Lisa started shaking as if she was about to urinate on herself. The unknown man unlocked the chain to release one hand for her to use, and he turned around.

Lisa urinated in the bucket, thinking how she could escape, but she could not figure it out. She didn't know where she was; there was not one door or window in sight. After she urinated, the unknown man left leaving one arm free.

Lisa sat rocking back and forth in a fetal position, with her arm still chained to the pole. She then pulled the food and water towards her feet. Lisa ate her food like she had never eaten before.

"God, please, if you are listening, please send someone for me, please," said Lisa as she prayed and ate her food.

A couple of days passed; Lisa's abandoned car was found on the road by Sergeant. McCanon, he knew something was wrong when he saw the trunk open, but nobody was there. When he exited his vehicle to see what happened, he noticed broken glass on the ground.

He walked closer, looked inside the car, and saw a female's bag. Sergeant. McCanon called it in for possible abduction.

When Sergeant. McCanon opened the car door to get the bag; he saw a cell phone on the floor. There were twenty-two missed calls and eighteen text messages.

Sergeant. McCanon could not see who the

calls and texts were coming from because it only captured Lisa's identity.

Sergeant. McCanon found Lisa's driver's license in her bag while on the phone with an agent from the missing persons' unit. He gave Lisa's first and last name so the agent could search the database.

Lisa's name didn't come up.

While awaiting the crime scene unit to arrive, Sergeant. McCanon wrote Lisa's address down so he could stop by to possibly get some answers. When he arrived at Lisa's home, Kim was sitting on the stairwell crying.

"Hello, Ma'am, I am Sergeant. McCanon, do you live here?" he asked.

"No, Sergeant, but my best friend does. I tried calling and knocking on the door, but no answer. I have not seen or heard from her in days." Kim started to agonize.

"Ma'am, I found an abandoned car over on 57th and Butler Rd," said Sergeant. McCanon.

"What color is the car…? Do you know how long it has been there?" asked Kim.

"No, ma'am, but the crime scene unit will investigate, and the color is silver." replied Sergeant. McCanon.

"Oh no, that's Lisa's car!" shouted Kim, as she covered her mouth; she was startled after hearing the car's color.

"I also found her bag, cell phone, and

driver's license, which is how I found the address," said Sergeant. McCanon.

"I should have stayed with her. . .we came together. . .we should have left together. . . I should not have left her. It's my fault. I am so stupid," said Kim.

"Ma'am, what happened…?

Calm down, tell me what happened?" asked Sergeant. McCanon while he pulled out his notepad to take notes.

"*We left a party, stopped at the gas station to get a bottle of water, and a friend of mine pulled up beside us and offered to take me home so Lisa could go straight home and not have to take me, and when I got home, I called Lisa, as she told me to do, but I didn't get an answer. I*

called many times. I also sent text messages, but

she has not responded since that day, I should

not have let her drive home alone. It's all my

fault. Do you think someone abducted her?"

asked Kim as she kneeled and wept to Sergeant.

McCanon.

"Ma'am, we are going to find your friend.

Come, get up now. Everything is going to be all

right. I do not know what happened, but we will

find out. I would like you to come to the station

to write a statement about that night," said

Sergeant. McCanon as he helped Kim stand up

on her feet.

"Do you think she's still alive?" Kim asked as she continued to weep.

"Does Lisa stay here alone…? Does she have any parents?" asked Sergeant. McCanon.

"No, Lisa's parents died in a car crash when she was younger, and her grandmother took care of her until she passed a few months ago. Lisa's grandmother left her in charge of everything.

Sergeant, you must find my friend. She's not a bad person. She doesn't deserve this. Please, Sergeant, please," said Kim as the tears rolled down her face.

When Kim and Sergeant. McCanon reached the station; Kim wrote a statement, and Sergeant McCanon put in a report with the missing

persons' unit. Immediately, Sergeant. McCanon started working on the case. He was determined to find Lisa.

Sergeant. McCanon had a daughter of his own in high school, so this case made him feel even more sympathetic.

He worked day and night, and even when the other officers on the case stopped to go home, he continued to put the puzzle pieces together to find Lisa.

The next day, Sergeant. McCanon and a dozen officers and search dogs searched all over town. Lisa was nowhere to be found.

They continued to search day and night until they came across a house in the back of a lonely road.

Sergeant. McCanon knocked on the door several times—no answer until he walked away.

"May I help you?" asked the elderly lady as she stood in the doorway.

"Yes, I am looking for a missing person." Sergeant. McCanon replied as he turned around to walk towards the elderly lady.

"Have you seen this young lady?" Sergeant. McCanon asked as he showed Lisa's picture.

"No, I did not," she replied.

"Thank you, Ma'am," said Sergeant. McCanon as he took a glance inside of the elderly lady's home.

He noticed some dingy boots.

"Are these your two cars, ma'am?" Sergeant. McCanon asked when he turned away to leave.

"They belong to my son, but he's asleep," said the elderly lady.

"Is it okay if I swing by a little later to talk with your son?" he asked.

"Sure," responded the elderly lady while closing her door.

Sergeant. McCanon felt something was not right. He walked over to the officers; they were searching the back of the house and in the bushes.

"Did you find anything?" he asked.

"No, boss," responded the officer. Sergeant.
McCanon and the officers left. Something did
not sit right with him; he continued to look back
at the house while walking away.

Sergeant. McCanon and the officers
continued to search, door to door, from house to
house. No sign of Lisa, and no one saw her.
Lisa's picture appeared on television two days
later for missing persons.

Suddenly, the unknown man's cup fell from
his hand, horrified seeing her picture, as he sat
looking at the television screen, scared to death,
not knowing what was going to happen next.

Surprisingly, there was a knock at the door *Boom-Boom-Boom.* The unknown man jumped out of his seat and tiptoed to the window to peep through the curtains to see who was knocking at the door. To his surprise, it was Sergeant. McCanon. He was timid; he rushed to the table to clean up his beer spill and turned the television off.

"How are you doing today, officer...? How may I help you?" The unknown man asked with fear in his eyes when he opened the door.

"Do you mind if I come in?" asked Sergeant. McCanon. "Do you have a warrant?" replied the unknown man.

"Do I need a warrant…? Are you hiding something?" asked Sergeant. McCanon in a sarcastic way. "No, officer−"

"Sergeant. to be exact," said Sergeant. McCanon as he interrupted the unknown man from talking.

"My apologies, officer, I-I-I mean, I'm sorry, Sergeant." said the unknown man, fidgeting while talking.

Sergeant. McCanon knew something was not right about this man. He asked one more time to come in. The unknown man extended his hand to make way for Sergeant. McCanon to enter.

"Thank you, Sir," said Sergeant. McCanon as he walked into the house.

"Have you seen this girl around?" asked Sergeant. McCanon as he showed Lisa's picture to the unknown man.

"Ah, no. Sergeant. I haven't seen her anywhere," the unknown man replied as he scratched his head.

"Okay," said Sergeant. McCanon as he tapped the picture against his hand and stared at the unknown man as if he knew he was lying.

"You have a nice place here; you stay here alone?" Sergeant. McCanon asked while walking around the living room.

"My-my-my-mother lives here," said the unknown man as he stuttered to get the word 'my' out. Sergeant. McCanon walked around, but when he stepped near the wall, he heard a creaking sound on the floor.

The unknown man reached to grab the beer bottle on the table in case he needed to react in a vicious way.

"You need to get that fixed," Sergeant. McCanon said as he turned around.

The unknown man quickly put the bottle down.

"If you happen to see this young lady. . . give me a call," said Sergeant. McCanon as he turns around to give the unknown man his business card.

Before leaving, Sergeant. McCanon froze in front of the door as if something came over him.

"Let me get that for you, Sarge," said the unknown man as he grabbed the doorknob to let Sergeant. McCanon out.

"You take care now," said Sergeant. McCanon as he exited the unknown man's house.

The unknown man was afraid. He did not know what else to do but huff, puff, and hit his head while pacing the floor. He was confused. He then walked over to the wall. After tapping the floor, he then tapped the wall for it to open.

The unknown man went into the cave. Lisa was lying down on the floor; she looked helpless.

He stood in front of her with a scowling look.

The unknown man left the cave, went to the gas station, and saw Lisa's *missing person's* picture everywhere. He was afraid; he panicked, following up at the liquor store next door from the gas station.

He bought a gallon of liquor to drink; after returning home, he sat at the table, turned the television on, and Lisa's picture was flashing across the screen.

The unknown man threw the remote control, hit the television, and started drinking his life away, feeling disgusted for abducting Lisa, more so afraid of getting caught.

"Why did I do it….? Why did I do it?" he questioned while hitting his head multiple times in one sitting, pacing the floor.

He then started to have flashbacks of when he was younger, about how his deceased father put him into the cave and left him there for days without eating or drinking anything until his mother would bring him food to eat. It seemed as if the unknown man was reliving his life; Instead, he abducted Lisa. He continued to drink his liquor, hit his head, and paced the floor until he could not anymore.

A day later, the elderly lady walked downstairs and saw her son stretched out on the dining room floor.

She thought he was too drunk and passed out because the liquor bottle was empty, not thinking he could be dead—she left him there and walked past as if he was invisible, not knowing he drank himself to death.

The unknown man was a beer, not a liquor drinker. That evening, he overdid it. The unknown man was gone sadly, unbeknown to his mother.

Sergeant. McCanon continued thinking about the feeling he had at the house. They continued to search day in and day out. There was no sign of Lisa.

Sergeant. McCanon thought to stop by the house again, unsure if he would get in this time without a warrant. Not knowing, the unknown man is dead.

"911, what is your emergency?" asked the 911 operator.

"MY SON! MY SON! I THINK HE'S DEAD!" shouted the elderly lady in a quavering voice, yet boisterous.

"Ma'am, tell me what happened?" responded the 911 operator.

"I don't know, he's just lying there," responded the elderly lady.

"Ma'am, can you check to see if he is responsive?" said the 911 Operator.

"No, please come, hurry." said the sobbing elderly lady as she hung up the phone on the 911 operator.

"Okay, ma'am, we will send someone over, *ma'am-ma'am-hello-hello-ma'am*." The 911 operator did not know the elderly lady had already hung up. Luckily, she called from a landline so they could trace the location.

"Charley... Char-ley," the elderly lady called on her son, known to her as Charley. She kicked him continuously, thinking he would get up, but still, he did not respond.

Charley was unresponsive.

Two officers and the paramedics arrived at the house. The paramedics announced Charley dead on arrival. Though Charley had been dead for some time, recognized by his *decomposing body smell*, the paramedics could not distinguish when it happened or how, but he was dead.

It was up to the medical examiners to provide the actual cause and time of death.

The coroner arrived to pick up Charley's body.

Sergeant. McCanon arrived as they were leaving.

He was puzzled—he couldn't understand what happened, but he thought it could have been Charley drinking himself to death due to the empty gallon bottle of liquor on the table. He then went looking for Charley's mom—she was nowhere to be found until he went upstairs, only to find that Charley's mom was in the rocking chair with her eyes open—dead as if she experienced a heart attack.

Sergeant. McCanon called it in. The officers, paramedics, and the coroner had to return to the home for Charley's mom.

"This is a nightmare," said Sergeant. McCanon as he walks down the stairs.

He looked around to figure things out while he waited for the coroner to pick up Charley's mother's body. Two dead bodies in the same household in one night. Sergeant. McCanon was stunned.

Suddenly, the same feeling he felt when he was there last time, came over him. He walked around but could not find anything that would help him understand the feeling he was having.

Sergeant. McCanon picked up the broken remote control off the floor in front of the television—he then looked up and realized the picture on the screen was blurry and the word *missing* was visible, and after carefully looking, he figured out what was showing on the television screen before it froze. Sergeant. McCanon stood there trying to piece it all together.

The officers and paramedics arrived.

Sergeant. McCanon pulled one of the officers aside. "*I found this remote broken on the floor in front of the television as if someone threw it; I looked up, saw the program for missing persons, and every time I come here, to this house, I get this weird feeling, a feeling I can't explain, but the feeling is unusual, something isn't right. I'm thinking, perhaps, the deceased, the man Charley, had something to do with the girl's disappearance.*

I have been sitting here trying to put the pieces together, but I can't quite put my finger on it. However, it seems Charley saw the girl's picture posted everywhere, watched it flashing on the television screen, and knew that we were on to finding her and soon he would get caught. He drinks himself to death, and here we are— this is the only thing I can come up with, but if he did have something to do with her going missing, where did he put her...?

That's the question... Where could she be....?

She's not here, " said Sergeant. McCanon as he expresses to the officer who listened attentively. Sergeant. McCanon continued to express his thoughts.

"Now, the mother, on the other hand, caught a heart attack and died because of her son—she could not fathom seeing him dead on the dining room floor. I know that must be the reason—I don't know for sure—but something is up." Sergeant. McCanon voiced his opinion with speculation, not knowing what happened with Charley and his mother, but he seemed right.

"I don't know, Sarge. You know we can't go off speculation, but it does sound weird, yet convincing," said the officer while trying to unravel what Sergeant. McCanon explained to him.

The night went unsolved; No evidence Charley did anything and no sign of Lisa.

After the coroners came to pick up the elderly lady's body, Sergeant. McCanon went home to sleep, he thought about the girl, what could have possibly happened and the two deaths that occurred today.

Kim and Sasha went to the precinct the next day to see Sergeant. McCanon.

"Any leads, Sergeant. McCanon?" asked Kim.

"Not yet, Miss Kim, we are still looking into the case. I have officers out now looking and posting up more flyers. We will find your friend; we are doing everything we can."

Sergeant. McCanon said, tempting to share with Lisa's best friends about how he felt when he went to Charley's house, thinking that Charley had something to do with their best friend missing, though he could not share any information about the case because his thoughts, and feelings were not a fact.

Almost three weeks later, Lisa's body still has not been found. Her helpless body was hanging on. She had eaten the food and drank all the water Charley gave her. Lisa prayed continually for someone to find her and not to die suffering.

Kim and Sasha went to the precinct daily to ask about her.

Though Sergeant. McCanon could not stop thinking about how a girl could vanish so suddenly in a small town with not an ounce of evidence to help lead him to find her.

Sergeant. McCanon started having nightmares. He would wake up in night sweats over someone he did not know. The nightmares and unusual feelings made him want to investigate even more.

Sergeant. McCanon decided to talk to his Captain about what he was going through and how he thinks the deceased—Charley had something to do with a missing person. His Captain gave him the green light to dig deeper into the case.

Sergeant. McCanon started asking around to see the video cameras in the area where they found Lisa's car. One camera nearby was not successful because it was too dark. He decided to go to the gas station to see their cameras. On the camera, it showed Charley in and out of the store every day.

"I need you to go to the date of April 22nd," he told the store clerk. The store clerk went to the date. Sergeant. McCanon saw Charley in the video, looking towards the counter.

He noticed a female at the counter but did not know if it was Lisa—the face looked different from her driver's license.

"Can you send me a copy of this video?" asked Sergeant. McCanon.

"Yes, I can send it to you now," responded the store clerk.

"Here is my card…the email address is on there," said Sergeant. McCanon. Everyone in the area was concerned about the missing person.

Sergeant. McCanon went back to the precinct. He called Kim to come and look at the video to see if it was Lisa waiting to pay for an item at the counter.

When Kim and Sasha arrived, they were happy to hear that, Sergeant. McCanon did not give up on finding Lisa.

"Any good news, Sergeant?" asked Kim when she saw him.

"I think I have something," he responded, as he showed the video. "Is that your best friend?"

"Yes, that's Lisa," said Kim and Sasha simultaneously.

"Do you see this right here…? Have you seen this man before?" Sergeant. McCanon asked as he pointed to Charley in the video.

"No," said Sasha.

"I have, Sergeant…he almost caused an accident with me and Lisa on the way home from school one day," said Kim.

"AHHHH… Sergeant. McCanon said as he snapped his fingers…

I knew it, I knew it, I just knew it," said Sergeant. McCanon. He was distraught.

Sergeant. McCanon felt he was getting somewhere and could have worked harder on the case from the beginning based on the nightmares and vibes he got at Charley's house.

Sergeant. McCanon told his Captain about the video and what Kim told him about Charley. There was not much he could do because Charley was dead. The only option was to go back to Charley's house to figure it all out. Now that no one was living there, Sergeant. McCanon thought it would be easier to get in without a warrant and conduct a search.

"You ladies go home. I will be working on this and will call you if anything," said Sergeant. McCanon as if he was up to something.

"You think they are going to find Lisa?" asked Sasha.

"I do, that Sergeant seems to care…we are not giving up on Lisa, even if we have to keep coming down here or calling every day," said Kim.

"You think she's still alive after all this time?" Sasha asked Kim as they were getting into the car.

"I don't know Sash. I hope so. You know Lisa, though, she is strong, and if God is listening to her prayers, I know Lisa is okay.

Somebody will find her. You know Lisa, she already has a relationship with the creator, so I'm sure wherever she is, she is hanging on," said Kim.

"God, please, let Lisa be okay," said Kim as she looked up. "Amen," said Sasha and Kim as they drove away.

Sergeant. McCanon and a few other officers went back to Charley's home. When they arrived, he noticed a different car in the driveway. He was confused; he did not think someone would be there. Sergeant. McCanon thought no one was home, but when he knocked on the door, to his surprise, a man, his wife, and three-year-old son came to the door.

"Hello, officer. How may I help you on this beautiful day?" said the man.

"It's Sergeant, but when did you all move in?" Sergeant. McCanon asked confusingly.

"Earlier today. We were trying to unpack and settle in. We saw the sign off the highway, called the number, and my wife and I got it for a good price; we are thankful for this house. It came right on time; it beats us staying in a hotel trying to find a place to live. Seems like this home was waiting for us; you know we are not from here. We are from Texas." The man said, smiling.

"Do you mind if I come in and talk with you both for a second?" Sergeant. McCanon asked.

"Sure, Sergeant," the man replied.

"Wow, everything still looks and feels the same," muttered Sergeant. McCanon, as he looked around. "I didn't think the property would sell so fast," he said as he locked his eyes on the man and his wife.

"Is everything okay, Sergeant?" asked the man as he grabbed his wife and pulled her into his arm.

"Uh…we have been searching for a missing person in the neighborhood, and I was just wondering, can we check your home and the outside area?" asked Sergeant. McCanon.

"Yes, anything I can do to help, Sergeant," the man replied while rubbing his wife's shoulders to make her feel at ease.

"Well, let's start upstairs." Sergeant. McCanon said while walking up the steps.

Sergeant. McCanon looked in all three bedrooms, no sign of Lisa. There was one room that stood out to him mostly; he started having flashbacks of seeing Charley's mother's dead body in the rocking chair. He remembered everything from that night. He continued to walk around, and still, there was no sign of Lisa.

The sounds of the homeowner's son dribbling his basketball on the floor; Sergeant. McCanon caught it after it rolled near him; he stepped forward and heard the floor creak like before.

He then stared in disbelief, wondering why the rest of the house did not creak, only in that area. Something was not right, Sergeant. McCanon thought to himself. He gave the ball back to the three-year-old and smiled.

"Thank you, Sir and Ma'am, welcome to the neighborhood. My officers and I will check the rest of the area. You all have a good day," said Sergeant. McCanon, leaving out with a soft smile.

"*Doggy, woof-woof,*" the three-year-old said as he saw the dogs with the officers.

Sergeant. McCanon, the officers, and their dogs went around back; they searched the whole area.

"*Ruff-ruff-ruff,*" the dogs started barking loudly near the hole in the ground behind the house.

Sergeant. McCanon used his flashlight to see if he could see anything, but there was nothing but water. The dogs then stopped barking. They were all confused.

"Why would the dogs bark and then stop…? Hmm, that was weird." Sergeant. McCanon asked one of the officers confusingly.

"Something is down there; the dogs didn't bark for nothing…but how do we get in the hole…it's too small for anyone to fit," said Sergeant. McCanon, as he walked over to the tree to get a long branch to stick into the hole.

"It feels like a wall at the bottom…a blockage…this tree branch cannot go any further…I wonder where this hole leads. The house does not have a basement, and behind here, there are a lot of bushes and trees," said Sergeant. McCanon, while sticking the branch in and out of the hole.

The officers and Sergeant. McCanon was muddled; they did not know what to do. They ended up leaving.

"I don't know Sarge. That's unusual," replied the officer.

Sergeant. McCanon was terrified. He had to figure out his next move. He knew Charley had something to do with Lisa's abduction, and he also felt close to finding what happened, but he just could not put his finger on exactly where she could be.

He continued to look back while walking away. Something was not right, he thought. The new homeowners stared out the window while he, the officers, and their dogs departed from the home. The three-year-old boy continued to play with his ball, and Lisa was still in the cave, getting weaker and weaker by the day.

Lisa's helpless body. She could not keep her eyes open, and she gradually drifted off. Suddenly, she heard a soft voice, "Lisa, wake up, wake up Lisa, it's not your time, get up, someone is coming." The soft voice whispered in Lisa's ear.

"Mama," Lisa said as she fought her eyes to open. Lisa saw her mom and dad's soul as if they were there staring back at her in physical form. Lisa jumped up like she saw a ghost, though she did, but because Lisa was out of it, her loved ones reminded her that it was not her time, and she needed to get up. Lisa started to cry, praying and praying more, asking God to help her.

Later that evening, Sergeant. McCanon went home to search the internet for information about Charley, the home, who owned it, and the reason for the hole in the ground. He could not understand why the officers' dogs barked and then stopped. He also couldn't understand the nightmares he started to have and the feeling that came over him every time he went into Charley's home—now belonging to the new homeowners.

In 1862, the house was built and owned by a wealthy family. They took in other families who could not protect themselves from being in an unsafe town.

When the owners died in 1903, one of the hidden families took over.

Sergeant. McCanon continued to read and noticed one of the hidden families was wealthy too—they were the parents of Charley's father. When Charley's grandparents passed, they left the house to Charley's parents.

Sergeant McCanon continued to search the internet; the cave was in the article, but there were no details about the location or the reason for the hole in the ground. It was strange.

Sergeant. McCanon continued to read the article, and it stated that Charley's grandfather was a great worker with his hands, incredibly good at building anything.

He taught Charley's father.

When Charley's grandfather passed, Charley's father took over and rebuilt the home but did not touch the cave. The cave at the time was where he put Charley. When Charley was born, his father was upset; he didn't want any children; he didn't want Charley around him. So, when Charley was old enough to talk, he started putting him in the cave.

Sergeant. McCanon couldn't believe what he was reading. Charley had to deal with being unwanted by his father, yet a mother who adored him. For every chance she had, she tried her best to fight Charley's father for putting their son in the cave, but she did not win.

Charley would sometimes spend days in the cave; his mother would sneak food for him to eat on nights when his father would come home highly intoxicated, and that was almost every night. When Charley turned thirteen-years-old, his father died from drinking too much. He no longer had to worry about the cave, but it hindered him from moving on with his life. He never forgave his father for what he did.

Therefore, it was the cause of his behavior and how he treated Lisa; seeing her picture on the television screen before he drank himself to death reminded him of everything his father used to do to him, and it bothered him; he became scared of getting caught but now after reading the article, Sergeant. McCanon felt like he was on to something; his mindset was everywhere. He was trying to figure it all out until he realized Lisa could be in the house in the cave, but where? He thought. The article didn't say.

Sergeant. McCanon banged his balled-up fist on the table in rage because he did not know exactly where the cave could be. He searched all through the house. He knew this could also be why Charley drank himself to death because he had something to do with Lisa going missing, though it seems Charley did what his father did to him.

The next day Sergeant. McCanon went to the house to see if the new homeowners could let him search their home again, but no one was there.

He walked around the house to see if he could come up with anything, but he could not find any clues as to where a hidden cave might be.

"*Ring-Ring-Ring*." Sergeant. McCanon pulled the phone out of his jacket to answer.

"Anything yet, Sergeant?" asked Kim.

"Not yet, but I think I am getting close." Sergeant. McCanon said as he seemed preoccupied with something else.

"That is good to hear, Sergeant, but what makes you think you are getting close?" asked Kim.

"Ma'am, I will keep you posted, just hang tight... I do not want to tell you anything that I am unsure of. Although, I do believe that I am closer to finding your best friend now than I was before... Just sit tight. I will keep you posted." Sergeant. McCanon calmly said.

"Thank you, Sergeant. Have a great day," said Kim as she hung up the phone.

Sergeant. McCanon wanted to wait for the new homeowners to return home, but he had to return to the precinct.

Before leaving, he decided to leave his card on the door knocker with the words in capital letters, *PLEASE CALL*.

It was now going on for a month; Lisa was still missing. She continued to pray with the weak strength she had and remembered the voices of her mom and dad telling her to wake up because someone was coming. Lisa stared at the wall, hoping and praying someone would walk through to save her from dying. She was on the verge of giving up, yet she was still fighting.

Later that night, Sergeant. McCanon had another nightmare; he jumped up to the sounds of his phone ringing.

"*Ring-Ring-Ring.*"

"Sergeant. McCanon speaking," he
answered.

"Sergeant. McCanon, we have something
you need to see. Please hurry," said the man's
wife, in a frightening voice.

"I am on my way," responded Sergeant.
McCanon as he rushed to put his clothes on to
head over to see what was going on.

When Sergeant. McCanon arrived; he saw
the wall cracked open like a door.

"*THIS IS THE CAVE; THIS IS THE CAVE!*"
he shouted with a smile filled with excitement to
find the cave.

"What cave, Sergeant?" asked the man and his wife.

"I believe one of my missing persons is in that cave… How did you get this to open?" Sergeant. McCanon asked while he was calling his Captain.

"My son and I were bouncing the ball, and I heard a creaking sound as he moved, and then I threw the ball towards him; he didn't catch it, so it hit the wall, then it just cracked open, but I was afraid to open it wider to see what was down there because it's so dark," said the man, while being interrupted by Sergeant. McCanon.

"Captain, I am at the new homeowners' house, and there is a cave here.

I don't know how far it goes, but it's in this house." Sergeant. McCanon exclaimed.

"Okay, sit tight… I am on the way. I will send for backup," said the Captain.

"But, Cap, the girl could be in there dead… I can go," said Sergeant. McCanon.

"Wait, for backup...and that is an order," said the Captain in a stern voice.

"All right, Captain." Sergeant. McCanon replied.

"Well, what did he say…are you going in there….? Why are you waiting?" asked the man's wife.

"My Captain gave me an order to wait for backup." Sergeant. McCanon said disappointedly.

The woman walked away and came back with two flashlights.

"You said a missing girl could be here; she could be dead or dying, and if we wait for backup, we can miss our chance of saving her life," she said.

Sergeant. McCanon was hesitating because he never disobeyed his Captain's order.

However, this was something he did not want to regret. He thought he was doing the right thing; he made an intuitive decision that was more important than his job.

He followed behind the man and did not wait for backup

"Ma'am, the police are on their way. Please let them in when they arrive. I am going after your husband," said Sergeant. McCanon as he clicked on his flashlight and went into the dark cave.

Sergeant. McCanon and the man entered the dark and eerie cave with a flashlight illuminating the long pathway, refusing to look back because it was pitch black. As they walked to the end, there was an open door. They went through with the hope of finding Lisa.

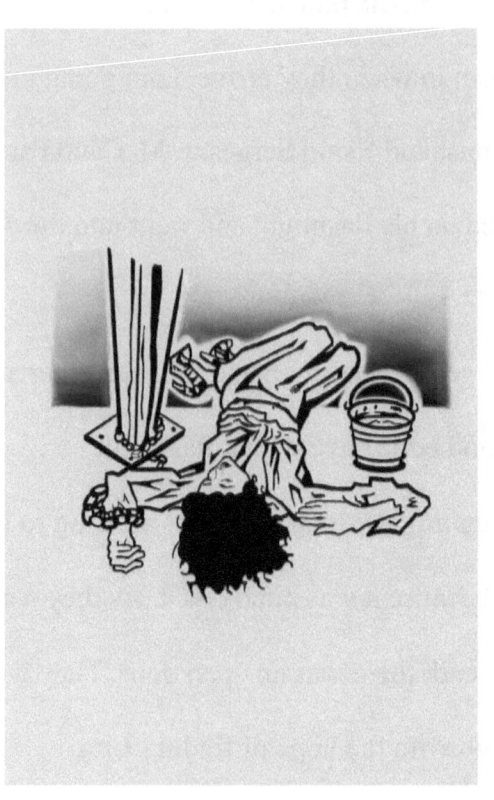

When they saw that the room was empty, they continued to walk. They walked through another door—it was empty, no Lisa. They continued to walk with their flashlights to see and ended up in a connected room without another door—they were baffled.

Sergeant. McCanon remembered that it could be another revolving door that appeared to be a wall like in the house.

"Let's check the walls to make sure, before we leave," said Sergeant. McCanon.

They walked lightly in front of the four walls in the room as they flashed their lights, but there were no creaking sounds until Sergeant. McCanon noticed a corner wall. He took one step towards it and heard a creaking sound. He flashed his light and saw an open crack in the wall, pushed it lightly, and realized it was a door as he pushed it open some more, flashing their lights, only to find Lisa's unconscious body on the floor next to a pail.

Sergeant. McCanon was shocked to see her and yet scared she could be dead. After checking her, he found out that she had a pulse, but it was weak.

"Let's get her body in the house so I can perform CPR, and you call 911 if the officers haven't arrived," said Sergeant. McCanon while moving frantically.

They picked up Lisa's unconscious body and ran with her out of the cave into the house, where the paramedics, officers, and the Captain were currently walking through the door.

The paramedics immediately went into action, putting Lisa on the stretcher, connected her to an IV pump, managed her airways, and performed chest compressions all at the same time.

Before Lisa arrived at the hospital, her pulse went up, and her heartbeat was normal.

"*Whew*, we made it just in time," said one of the paramedics, as she smiled at her colleagues because they just saved a life.

Sergeant. McCanon followed the paramedics to the hospital. When he saw that Lisa was okay, he called Lisa's best friend, Kim.

Kim then called Sasha, and they went to the hospital and stayed by Lisa's bedside until she woke up the next day.

Lisa's best friends were happy she did not die; despite her being close to it, she gave it her all and did not give up.

"Lisa, I am so sorry I left you; this was all my fault. I should've stayed. I should not have let you go home by yourself at that time of night—I am so sorry, Lisa, I am so sorry. I will never leave you again," said Kim as she wept.

"It's okay, don't cry, I am here now—It's not your fault. I blame myself... It's a lesson learned for all of us. *Never drive home alone on the road after leaving a party so late. Always take someone with you or have someone you know come pick you up because anything can happen. Next time, we'll take a rideshare to get home, plan a sleepover, and your cell phone goes with you whenever you leave the car, even if you are only getting gas*," said Lisa.

The girls laughed and embraced each other with a group hug like always.

While Kim and Sasha were in Lisa's arms hugging her, she looked up, smiled, and said, "*Thank you, God.*"

Later that day, Sergeant. McCanon went to check on the new homeowners after what happened last night. He knocked on the door, and they were waiting to welcome him.

"How is she?" they asked.

"She is doing fine… How are you both doing?" Sergeant. McCanon asked in concern.

"We are doing good, just wondering about the girl," said the man and wife.

"Good to hear… Thank you for helping save a life," said Sergeant. McCanon as he grinned and walked towards the door.

"Anytime, Sergeant," said the man and wife as they waved goodbye.

"What a wonderful feeling," said Sergeant. McCanon. He was elated.

It was then, Sergeant. McCanon knew why he felt weird in that house when he went in. There was something wrong, and that something was Lisa–*THE GIRL IN THE CAVE*.

The mystery unraveled, and the weird feeling went away.

The End.

"The lessons we learn in life can become helpful

for the days to come."

~Tomika Y. Reid

About the Author

Tomika Reid is a native of Brooklyn, New York. She is a mom of two daughters and a self-published author. Tomika has been through many trials and tribulations, yet she is here STILL STANDING and loves to inspire and motivate others to push through no matter what they go through.

The losses of her mom, sister, grandmother, and first and second daughters' fathers left her heartbroken. Tomika wanted to give up many times, but the love of her daughters and God kept her going.

Tomika's first book, "Nicolli and the Shining Star," is a children's book to help a children cope with the loss. Tomika self-published this book on behalf of her daughters because of the loss of their fathers. Many people told Tomika that her story needed to be told. After receiving confirmation to write her second book, a memoir titled, "Beyond the tears I've cried here I am Still Standing," she self-published to help, inspire, and encourage others to NEVER GIVE UP.

Tomika wanted others to see she was a living testimony who didn't give up so they could be inspired and motivated to never give up too and to also know, "You Are Not Alone."

In November 2014' Tomika received a Certificate of Appreciation for presenting at the General Membership Meeting from The Association of Black Educators of New York. She also conducted a Literary Workshop in Brooklyn, New York.

Tomika has appeared on several podcasts and television shows, which include Atlanta Live, This Day with BJ Arnett on Atlanta's Channel 57, The G Wade Radio Show, Energy Toss Radio Show, The Sylbourne Sydial Show in the UK, The Lekeisha Mosley Show on Atlanta's Channel 25, FOX Soul's The Book of Sean, and Featured on The Tamron Hall Show.

Tomika has conducted a reading at the Atlanta

Children's Shelter. She was an extra in the movie "Nobody's Fool" by Tyler Perry and a guest on multiple Blog Talk Radio Shows. Tomika was also a contributor for The Spin Awards Magazine, featured in VoyagerATL Magazine and The Source Magazine for her first children's book.

Tomika has conducted readings at several Libraries and Day Care Centers in Brooklyn, New York, and Atlanta, Georgia.

In March 2020' Tomika self-published her third book titled, "Inspire your way through The Storm," a quote and poem guidebook to inspire you through the storms you face today for a better tomorrow.

[Audiobook is available on Audible.com]

In December 2020' Tomika self-published her fourth book titled, "Suzie sings, this is the color," a children's book to help children learn the main colors in a fun way by singing a song—what a way to LEARN and SING!

In 2022' Tomika self-published her fifth book "Hello Beautiful," an uplifting tween and teen girl book. Later this year, the Associated Press of New York featured Tomika in a published story, and she was also a guest on News Nation's Morning in America and featured in an article in a local newspaper, The Monty News.

Tomika hopes to turn her memoir, "Beyond the tears I've cried here I am Still Standing," into a movie one day.

Tomika will continue writing, being an inspiration, and turning her dreams into a reality.

To order additional copies of this

book,

Contact:

Email: iyannaice11@gmail.com

Website: TomikaReid.com